Steck-Vaughn
POINT
of
VIEW
Stories

# The <sub>Un</sub>Fairest of Them All

*Underlined: Un*

# Them All

By
## Dr. Alvin Granowsky

*Illustrated by*
## Mike Krone

RSVP
**RAINTREE**
**STECK-VAUGHN**
P U B L I S H E R S
The Steck-Vaughn Company

*Austin, Texas*

**I**n spite of what you may have heard, all stepmothers are not wicked. Nor do we hate children. In fact, no one ever wanted a child more than I. Absolutely no one!

When I married the handsome and wealthy king and became his beautiful and wealthy queen, my first thought was, "How absolutely wonderful! Now I will become the stepmother of his lovely, little daughter who lost her own dear mother years ago."

She was such a precious little girl. Her hair was as black as ebony, her lips were as red as roses, and her skin was as white as snow. In fact, her skin was so lovely that she was named Snow White.

Who could have imagined that my dream of being a mother to this exquisite child would turn into a nightmare? An absolute nightmare!

At our very first meeting, I realized the little girl might have a problem accepting me. "Darling Snow White," her father said, "this enchanting lady is my new queen. She is now your mother. I love her, and I know you will come to love her, too."

I reached out my arms to hug the beautiful child. Snow White pulled back and stuck her tongue out at me. Then she looked directly into my eyes and said, "I don't want a stepmother!"

I smiled my most gracious, queenly smile and said, "With time, I know we will grow to love one another."

I turned to her father and whispered, "Some things do take time." I wanted him to know that I could understand his daughter's rude and unladylike behavior. The child, after all, had been raised without a mother's loving guidance. She needed the kind of gentle supervision that someone like me could provide.

Time passed. Months turned into years. Try as I might (and I truly did try), I never won Snow White's affection. I could do nothing to please the child. I gave her toys, and she threw them into the moat. I offered her candy, and she bit me. I complimented her, and she called me a liar. The more I tried to befriend her, the angrier she became. To her, I was an evil stepmother. Me? Evil and vicious? I should say not.

Anyone in the kingdom would tell you that I am a proper queen—gracious and gorgeous. I would say that being gorgeous is the most difficult part of the job. People tend to be jealous of someone who is as stunning as I am. Snow White was certainly jealous. Particularly where her father was concerned. When he would remark on my captivating good looks (which was often), Snow White would mutter under her breath, "Yeah, pretty as a prune and about as wrinkled."

Snow White's insults became unbearable when she began to accuse me of trying to kill her. "Why would you think such a thing?" I asked. "For heaven's sake, Snow White, what possible reason would I have for killing you? You really must stop this nonsense. People will start to talk. That's a ridiculous idea."

She persisted in telling those lies. I realized that she intended to convince my husband that I was a monster. I would soon find out just how determined she was to come between the king and me.

"Snow White," I continued, "I am your stepmother and I love you."

"Oh, you never loved me!" Snow White yelled in a nasty tone she reserved especially for talking to me. And now that I have grown more beautiful than you, you can't stand it!"

Then she ran to that magic mirror we had and asked:

> Mirror, mirror, on the wall
> Who's the fairest one of all?

And the mirror answered:

> The queen once was fairest,
> It is true.
> But now Snow White
> The fairest is you!

"See?" Snow White yelled. "I am the fairest in the land, and that's why you want to kill me. You can't stand to have a stepdaughter more beautiful than you. You are such a vain woman. I don't know why my father ever married you!"

I was stunned by her dreadful accusations. Because I am so attractive myself, beauty is a quality I admire in others. No one was more proud of Snow White's beauty than I. The things she said hurt me terribly. I had never given her any reason to be so vicious.

The worst part of this situation was what it was doing to her poor father, the king. The dear, sweet man was caught between the two of us. He loved me, but he loved his daughter, too. He wanted to please both of us and couldn't. He didn't know what to do or who to believe.

As if matters weren't bad enough, soon we received some terrible news—Snow White had run away! When the palace guard notified us that Snow White was gone, I asked, "Gone? What do you mean gone? Is she visiting friends at a neighboring castle? Is she traveling to some distant kingdom?"

There was a long, awkward pause. I remember looking at my husband to see if he knew what was going on. Then I looked back at the guards. When I spoke, my voice was choked with emotion. "Do you mean that she has left home? She doesn't plan to return?" I asked.

The guards nodded grimly, and I asked quite innocently, "But why would she run away? This is her home. This is where she's lived and been loved her whole life." The two guards looked at their feet and refused to answer. "Tell us at once!" I demanded. "Why has Snow White run away?"

One of the guards spoke up at last. "A rumor has spread throughout the kingdom that Princess Snow White fled for her life after a huntsman tried to kill her."

I was completely shocked by those words. The king said nothing. I looked at him in horror, waiting for him to order the huntsman to be hung. But he didn't utter a sound.

Eventually, I spoke up. "Is our beloved Snow White hurt? Did any injury befall her? If that huntsman harmed so much as . . . " and then I grew quiet. Why was everyone

eyeing me suspiciously? I began to feel very uneasy. "Who is this huntsman, and why did he want to kill the princess?" I demanded.

Finally, my husband spoke. "It's been said that you paid the huntsman to kill Snow White."

His words were like daggers through my heart. "Who could have said such a thing? Who would make up such lies?" And even as I asked the question, I knew the answer. There was only one person—the princess, Snow White.

I walked back to my chambers with a heavy heart. Snow White had succeeded at last. After all the years of trying, she had finally caused her father to doubt me. I could see it in his eyes. He believed that I meant his beloved daughter harm and had caused her to run away. I knew that soon he would learn to hate me and would regret that we had ever married. What could I do to save our marriage? How could I hold on to the man I loved?

I knew I must find Snow White and bring her back to live at the palace. It was the only way to prove my innocence and ease my beloved husband's pain.

To begin to solve our problems, I turned to the magic mirror and asked it the question it alone could answer:

> *Mirror, mirror, on the wall*
> *Where's the fairest one of all?*

To which the mirror replied:

> *Beloved queen, once most fair,*
> *You seek the one with ebony hair.*
> *She dwells within the wooded glen*
> *With the seven little men.*

That was just what I needed to know. I decided to go over there and straighten things out.

At first I thought of simply getting in my carriage and driving right out to the seven dwarfs' home. For starters I would demand that Snow White apologize to me for the ugly rumor she had spread throughout the kingdom. Then I would insist that she return home to her father and admit what she had done and why she had done it. The simple

truth was that Snow White had spread that rumor as a vengeful act to come between her father and me.

As soon as I calmed down, I realized that Snow White would never do what I was asking. She was an *exceptionally* headstrong young girl. I would never get her to admit her guilt, and I couldn't bring her back without the use of force. If I were to win our battle for the love of her father, I would have to resort to cunning, just as she was doing.

I came up with a strategy that I knew would work. I dressed up as an old peddler woman and went to the seven dwarfs' cottage when I knew they would be away at work. I knocked softly at the door. When Snow White answered, I said in a disguised voice, "Hello, my pretty, are you home all alone? Will you let me in? I have a beautiful, gold comb for you to wear in your lovely, black hair. Let me in, and I'll show you."

Before Snow White would open the door, I had to show her the gold comb.

"Yes, I do think I would like that," she said. She opened the door, and grabbed the comb from my hand.

"Oh, it's simply stunning!" Snow White put the comb in her hair. "Do I look beautiful in it? I am so much better looking than that evil queen who rules the kingdom. Do you know she is out to kill me because I have grown more beautiful than she is?" Snow White prattled on until I could stand it no more.

Hearing all those lies upset me to no end. I gave up disguising my voice and cried, "Snow White, you stop that! Stop it this very instant! As your stepmother, I am trying very hard to love you, but you are not making it easy. Think of your poor father. End this charade at once! Come back to the palace with me and—"

Snow White cut me off with her shrieking. "Oh, the evil queen! My wretched stepmother has come to kill me!" Then she began her dramatic play-acting. She fluttered her eyelids, fell to the floor, and pretended to be in a coma.

Try as I might, I could not get that stubborn girl to get up and talk to me. She was playing her act for all it was worth.

"You have put me in a coma!" she gasped. "As soon as I stop breathing, I will be dead. Now please return to the palace, and tell my father that you have killed me!"

A coma! I don't know where that young lady got such a vivid imagination.

"Please, Snow White! Please, don't do this to me!" I begged her to get up and return with me to the palace, but I may as well have been talking to a stone. When Snow White gets in one of those moods you can't do a thing with her. I had no choice but to leave her lying on the floor of the seven dwarfs' cottage.

I returned to the palace, my heart heavy with grief. I had done nothing to deserve this treatment. I had done everything I could think of to get the girl to come around, but still she resisted me.

I wanted to sit down beside my husband and tell him everything that had just happened. I wanted to seek his help. I wanted him to comfort me. But instead of consoling me, he added to my misery.

"It was wrong of me to take you as my wife," he said. "I'll never forgive myself for the suffering I've caused Snow White by marrying you!"

My heart sank at his words. I thought that things could not get any worse. But alas, I was wrong. Things could be worse, and soon they were, for I found out that the seven dwarfs were telling everyone in the kingdom that I had tried to murder Snow White. When a trusted servant told me that the ridiculous tale of the poisoned comb was being told throughout the kingdom, I almost fainted from despair. Who could believe there was such a thing as a poisoned comb? Why on Earth would I attempt to poison my very own stepdaughter? To hear the dwarfs tell it, Snow White was at death's door when they found her. What an actress! No wonder I was receiving such strange looks. People actually believed those terrible lies. No wonder my beloved husband was no longer talking to me. He believed those awful lies, too!

I desperately needed to talk to Snow White to try one more time to persuade her to end our differences. I still had no idea what I could have done to offend the girl, but I was willing to do anything to remedy the situation.

I knew Snow White would never allow me in, so I dressed myself up as a different old woman, even older and sweeter than the first. This time I was a farmer's wife with a basket of apples to sell.

As I stood at the door of the dwarfs' cottage I said, "I have a beautiful apple for you, my lovely. Please let this old lady in so I can give you this delicious fruit."

Snow White would not open the door. She peeked out the window. "I have to be especially careful who I let in," she confided, "as my stepmother, who is insanely jealous of my beauty, nearly killed me just the other day. The evil woman will not stop at anything to get me and . . . "

Again, I just couldn't take hearing those lies. I threw myself against the locked door and begged her to return with me to the palace. "Please, we must end our differences! Return home with me, and we will work everything out. Tell me what it is you want, and I will see that you get it."

Snow White's only words were, "Oh, no! It's you again! What have you brought to kill me with this time?"

"Now you stop that!" I yelled. "Snow White, I have never tried to harm you, and you know that perfectly well! A poisoned comb, indeed!"

She didn't answer outright, but her next sentence proved she had been lying. "Is that big, red apple for me?" she said, pointing to the biggest apple in my basket.

Now, would she have taken food from me if she believed I had tried to poison her?

"If you want the apple, you may have it," I said kindly. "Here, take it." I handed my stepdaughter the apple, and she took a bite of it.

"Oh, it's poisoned!" she screamed. "How trusting and stupid of me to have tasted anything you gave me!"

Once again, Snow White collapsed to the floor.

"You have put me in a coma!" she gasped. "As soon as I stop breathing, I will be dead. Now, please, return to the palace, and tell my father that you have killed me!"

There was no use trying to reason with her. I pleaded with her to end this deceit, but she wouldn't listen. She simply repeated, "You have put me in a coma. As soon as I stop breathing, I will be dead."

Finally, I returned to the palace. I might as well start packing my belongings, I thought. My marriage will be over, and in all likelihood, I will be banished from the kingdom for attempting to kill the princess.

Soon enough, the foolish tale spread throughout the kingdom. Silly peasants everywhere began to believe I had poisoned Snow White with an apple. The beautiful Snow White was lying in a coma in a glass casket that the seven dwarfs had built for her. What a convincing little act she was putting on! Getting herself laid out in a glass casket was a clever touch. I mean, that's some prop. It definitely had everyone convinced that I, motivated by jealousy of Snow White's beauty, had poisoned her. Can you imagine that? But words would never persuade anyone that I was innocent. I would have to do something to prove to everyone that Snow White was still alive.

I must show that, as her stepmother, I longed for her happiness, not her demise. Somehow I would have to bring Snow White much joy. But how? There was only one way: I would have to play matchmaker between Snow White and a charming prince. That was it! I would find a way to have a handsome, young prince come her way and fall in love with her. That would bring her out of her so-called coma—that much I knew.

Getting Snow White and a handsome prince together wasn't easy. In fact, it was the most difficult bit of arranging I have ever done. In a stroke of genius, I had an invitation engraved in silver and gold and sent to the prince of a neighboring kingdom.

You are cordially invited to pay your respects to
the beautiful Princess Snow White.
She is lying in a glass casket
on the dwarfs' hilltop
and will be buried
as soon as she stops breathing and dies.
Please arrive as promptly as possible
as your future happiness and hers
require that she still be breathing when you arrive.

Finally, I succeeded where Snow White was concerned! The charming prince arrived right on schedule to view Snow White in the casket.

"Oh, she is so beautiful," the handsome, young prince said. "She is the most beautiful girl I have ever seen. Am I too late? Is there no hope that she will live? To think that I have found my true love, and she may be lost to me forever!"

"Oh, handsome prince!" the seven dwarfs cried. "Our beautiful Snow White is in a coma. She has taken a bite from a poisoned apple and will die as soon as she stops breathing!"

"What a shame that she never lived to see you!" the eldest dwarf said. "You are so handsome and kind, I know she would have fallen in love with you and lived happily ever after in your kingdom far away from here!"

Well, what happened next showed I hadn't been Snow White's stepmother all those years without knowing something about the way that girl's head worked.

As the story is reported, Snow White opened one of her eyes. As soon as she saw how handsome the prince was, her other eye popped open, too. She faked a little cough and said, "That bit of poisoned apple is no longer caught in my throat." Then she batted her eyelashes at the prince.

"Oh, Snow White is alive!" the seven dwarfs sang out.

"Will you marry me, Snow White?" asked the handsome prince. "I will take you far away from here so that you will never have to see your horrible stepmother again. We will live happily ever after."

"Can my father come to visit me whenever he wants?" asked Snow White. "I'll make him promise to leave my stepmother back at the palace."

"Of course," said the prince . "I love you, Snow White, and I will do everything you want!"

"I love you, too," said Snow White. "And as long as you promise to do **everything** I want, I will marry you. Then we will live happily ever after."

So Snow White and the prince had the most beautiful wedding ever (according to all reports of those who were invited to the wedding, which was everyone in the kingdom except for me). I'm told that when my husband walked down the aisle with his daughter, he looked as proud as she looked radiant. He still can't see the **real** Snow White.

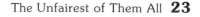

Snow White had made it very clear that this was her wedding day, and she wanted me to have no part of it. She made her father promise he would not bring me to the wedding. She claimed that my jealousy of her beauty in her bridal magnificence might cause me to try to kill her again, and naturally, that would not make for a happy wedding day. (Personally, I think she was afraid people would be looking at me instead of her.)

I told the king that I would honor his daughter's wish and stay home. Anything that would bring peace to the palace, once and for all, would be fine with me.

And so you see, no one will ever know the heartache I've been through in trying to be a mother to Snow White. And I'll never get the credit I deserve for arranging a life of happiness for that ungrateful girl.

So much for marrying a rich and handsome king to have the happiness of raising his beautiful daughter as your very own!

Steck-Vaughn
**POINT**
of
**VIEW**
*Stories*

# Snow White

## A Classic Tale

*Retold by*
Dr. Alvin Granowsky

*Illustrated by*
Rhonda Childress

RSVP

**RAINTREE**
**STECK-VAUGHN**
**P U B L I S H E R S**
The Steck-Vaughn Company

*Austin, Texas*

**O**n a winter's day long ago, in a faraway land, a queen sat sewing by an ebony-framed window. As she stitched, she glanced up to watch the snow drift down from the sky and pricked her finger with the needle. Three drops of blood fell onto the snow that had gathered on the windowsill. The queen thought about the beauty of the colors she saw and said to herself, "If only I had a child with lips as red as blood, skin as white as snow, and hair as black as this ebony window frame."

Soon afterward, the queen gave birth to such a child—a lovely, little princess with lips of rosy red, hair of deepest black, and skin so pure and fair that she was named Snow White. At the very moment the child was given life, the young queen lost hers.

Several years later, the king took another wife. The new queen was beautiful but haughty, proud, and vain. Indeed she was so vain that her heart's desire was to be the fairest in all the land. All day long she thought of nothing but her own beauty.

The queen possessed a magical mirror, and she delighted in its special powers. Each day she stood before the mirror and gazed at herself. And each day she would ask the mirror:

> *Mirror, mirror, on the wall*
> *Who's the fairest one of all?*

And the mirror would reply:

> *O queen, the fairest, it be true*
> *Can be no other one than you!*

The mirror's words made the queen smile with satisfaction, for she knew the mirror spoke the truth. Her satisfaction would come to an end, though, for Snow White grew more beautiful with each passing year. Throughout the kingdom people spoke of Snow White's loveliness and admired her gentle nature. Soon she was as fair as the day and even more beautiful than the queen.

The day came when the queen asked the mirror:

> *Mirror, mirror, on the wall*
> *Who's the fairest one of all?*

And the mirror replied:

> *Queen, thou art of a beauty rare,*
> *But Snow White is a thousand times*
> *more fair.*

With that the queen became furious. From that time on, she could look at Snow White with only hatred in her heart.

Each time the queen thought of Snow White's beauty, she was filled with jealousy. Finally she could bear it no longer. The queen called for her huntsman and said, "Take the child into the forest and do away with her. I never want to lay eyes upon her again. You must bring me a token so that I will know you have obeyed me. Bring back her heart."

The huntsman could not bear the thought of harming the dear princess, but he dared not disobey the queen.

So the huntsman took Snow White into the woods. His heart was heavy as he drew the knife to pierce life from the innocent child. Snow White wept and begged, "Dear huntsman, please spare my life! I promise to run into the wild and remain there forever!"

"Be gone then, poor child," said the huntsman. "May the beasts of the forest have mercy on you." Just then a wild boar ran past. The huntsman killed it and presented its heart to the queen, who accepted it as Snow White's.

Snow White was all alone in the great forest, terrified and unsure of what to do. She began to run and sent herself over jagged rocks and through thorny brambles. Wild animals raced past her but did her no harm. She ran until her feet could carry her no more.

At last she spied a little cottage and went inside to rest. Everything inside the cottage was small, charming, and very tidy. Snow White saw a table laid with a clean, white cloth and seven little place settings. She ate and drank a bit from each setting, as she did not want to take all from only one. Along one wall were seven little beds neatly made with white spreads. She laid down to rest on one of the little beds and fell fast asleep.

As darkness crept into the little house, so did the owners. They were seven dwarfs who dug for gold and gems in the mountains. They lit their seven little candles and saw Snow White lying on the bed.

The dwarfs were puzzled to find her there. So pleased were they with the beauty of their guest, they didn't even wake her but let her sleep through the night. In the morning Snow White was startled at the sight of the seven little men scurrying around. One of them spoke to her kindly. "What is your name?" he asked.

The gentle way the dwarf addressed her let Snow White know that the little men were friendly folk. "I am called Snow White," she replied.

"How is it that you are here?" asked the dwarfs.

Snow White told them her sad story. When she was finished, the dwarfs asked, "Would you like to take care of our house for us—cook, sew, wash our clothes, and

make our beds? If you will keep our home neat and clean, you may stay with us, and you will not want for anything."

"Oh, yes," said Snow White. "With all my heart, I want to stay with you."

And so she remained. Each day the dwarfs went up to the mountains to dig for gold and gems. While they were gone, Snow White cooked, cleaned, washed, and mended. Each evening the little men returned to a tidy house and a hot meal. The dwarfs came to love gentle Snow White and they wanted to protect her. The dwarfs bid her to be careful. "Beware of your stepmother, dear child. Soon she will learn where you live and will come looking for you. While we are away each day, take care and let no one in."

The dwarfs were right. Before long the queen stood before her mirror and asked:

*Mirror, mirror, on the wall*
*Who's the fairest one of all?*

Whereupon the mirror answered:

*Thou art fair, O lovely queen*
*But the fairest ever seen*
*Dwells within the wooded glen*
*With the seven little men.*

The queen was filled with anger. She knew that the mirror spoke the truth and that the huntsman had lied when he claimed to have killed Snow White. The queen immediately began to think of another plan to destroy Snow White. The wicked queen's heart would have no peace as long as the princess lived.

The queen disguised herself as an old peddler woman and set out to the seven dwarfs' with a poisoned comb in her basket. When she reached the cottage, she disguised her voice and called out, "Pretty things for sale!"

At this Snow White came to the door and said, "Good day! What are you selling?"

"Good things. Just look at this beautiful, gold comb."

Snow White did not suspect that the old lady or the beautiful, gold comb would harm her. She made a bargain for the comb and took it from the old woman. Scarcely had she put it into her beautiful, ebony hair when the poison worked, and Snow White fell down as if she were dead.

"Now you have what you deserve!" cried the wicked queen, and she was off.

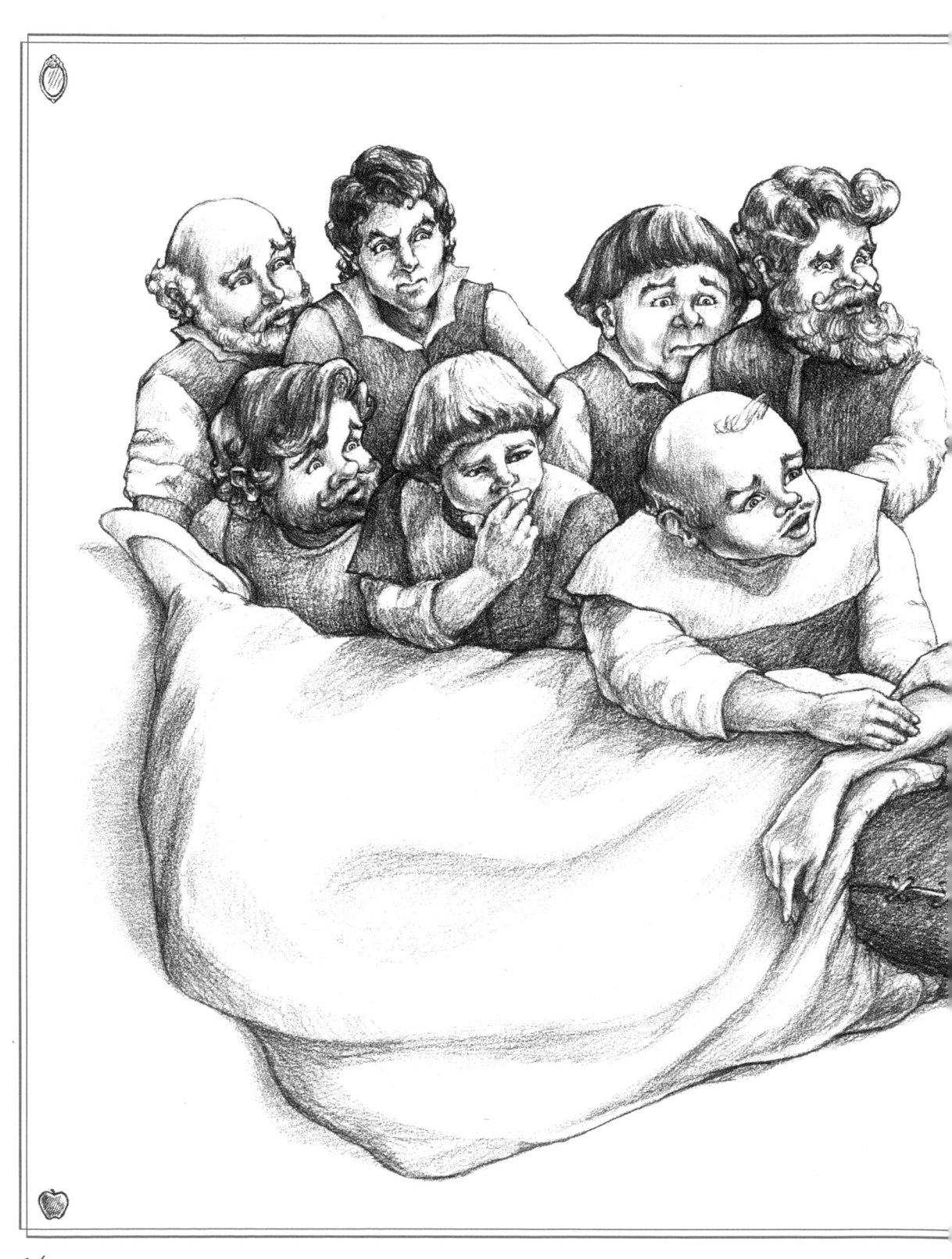

When the seven dwarfs came home, they found Snow White lying on the floor as if she were dead. The dwarfs searched her for signs of evil-doing, for they suspected the queen's mischief. When they took the strange, gold comb out of Snow White's hair, she recovered and told them what had happened.

When the queen returned to the palace, she stood before her mirror and asked:

> *Mirror, mirror, on the wall*
> *Who's the fairest one of all?*

The mirror answered as before:

> *Thou art fair, O lovely queen*
> *But the fairest ever seen*
> *Dwells within the wooded glen*
> *With the seven little men.*

The queen trembled with rage. "Snow White shall die!" she cried. "I **will** think of something that will be the end of her!"

Soon the queen was busy at her dreadful task of fashioning a poisonous apple. When she was finished, the apple appeared so pretty to all who saw it that they were possessed by a desire to eat it. It was so deadly, though, that whoever ate even a small bit of it would surely die.

Disguised as a farmer's wife, the queen packed the apple and set off for the dwarfs' cottage. When she reached their little house, she knocked at the door. Snow White peeked out the window and said, "I am not allowed to let anyone in or to buy anything. The seven dwarfs have forbidden me to do so."

"It's all the same to me," said the old woman. "I shall soon be rid of all my apples. Indeed, I'll even give you one."

"No," said Snow White. "I dare not accept anything from you."

"Are you afraid of poison?" asked the old woman. "See here." And she cut the apple in half. "I'll just have a bit of it myself."

The apple was so cleverly made that only half of it was poisonous.

Snow White longed for the fine apple, and when she saw that the peasant woman had eaten part of it, she could resist no longer. She reached out and accepted the poisoned half. No sooner had she taken a bite of it, than she turned pale and fell to the ground.

The queen let out an evil laugh and shouted, "As white as snow, as red as blood, as black as ebony—**now** let the dwarfs restore you!"

Once home, the queen stood before the magical mirror and asked:

> *Mirror, mirror, on the wall*
> *Who's the fairest one of all?*

And finally, to the fiendish queen's delight, the mirror replied:

> *O queen, the fairest, be it true*
> *Can be no other one than you!*

At last her envious heart could rest.

When the dwarfs trudged home in the evening, they again found Snow White lying on the floor. No breath came from her mouth, no beat from her heart. The dwarfs were full of woe, for they knew this to be the work of the wicked queen. They picked Snow White up and looked for something poisonous. They found no marks and nothing out of place. The dear child did not move, or speak, or open her eyes.

All seven dwarfs sat around her and wept for three solid days. At the end of the third day, they were going to bury her, but she still looked beautiful and full of good health.

"We cannot bury this beauty in the cold, dark earth," said the dwarfs.

The dwarfs had a glass casket made for Snow White so that she could be seen from all sides. It had her name written upon it in golden letters to show that she was a princess. The dwarfs gently laid Snow White inside the casket and carried it to the top of a hill, where they placed

it among trees and flowers. The dwarfs took turns keeping watch over Snow White. They were joined by creatures of the wood who came to mourn her—first an owl, then a raven, and finally a dove.

Much time passed and Snow White remained unmoving in the casket. She appeared to be in a deep, deep sleep. Her face was poised as if in the midst of a pleasant dream, and her cheeks were flushed their rosy red. Even the woodland beasts would come and admire the beautiful, young princess.

In time someone else came to gaze in wonder—not a deer, nor a squirrel, nor a bird, but a young prince who happened to be traveling through the forest. He saw the sleeping maiden, so beautiful and rosy, and read the golden letters. The prince spoke to the dwarfs. "Please let me have the casket. I will give you all the gold you desire," he said.

But the dwarfs answered, "We would not part with it for all the gold in the world."

"I see," said the prince. "Then please give it to me as a gift, for I cannot live without seeing Snow White. I will honor her with all my heart and guard her as my greatest treasure."

The dwarfs took pity on the prince and presented him with Snow White in her casket.

The prince was overjoyed and called his servants to carry Snow White to the castle. Gently, they hoisted her up and carried her on their shoulders. They happened to stumble over a creeping vine. The sudden movement freed the piece of poisoned apple from Snow White's lovely throat. She woke up and was as well as ever.

She looked about in astonishment and asked, "Where am I?"

The handsome prince rushed to her and lifted her from the casket. He told her all that had happened and then proposed. "I love you, Snow White, more than anything in this world. Will you come to my father's castle with me and be my bride?" he asked.

Snow White answered joyously, "Yes!" She, too, had fallen in love.

After their magnificent wedding, Snow White and the prince made their life far away from the evil queen's harm but close to the kindness of the seven dwarfs. The prince and Snow White ruled their kingdom with grace and good will and lived happily ever after.

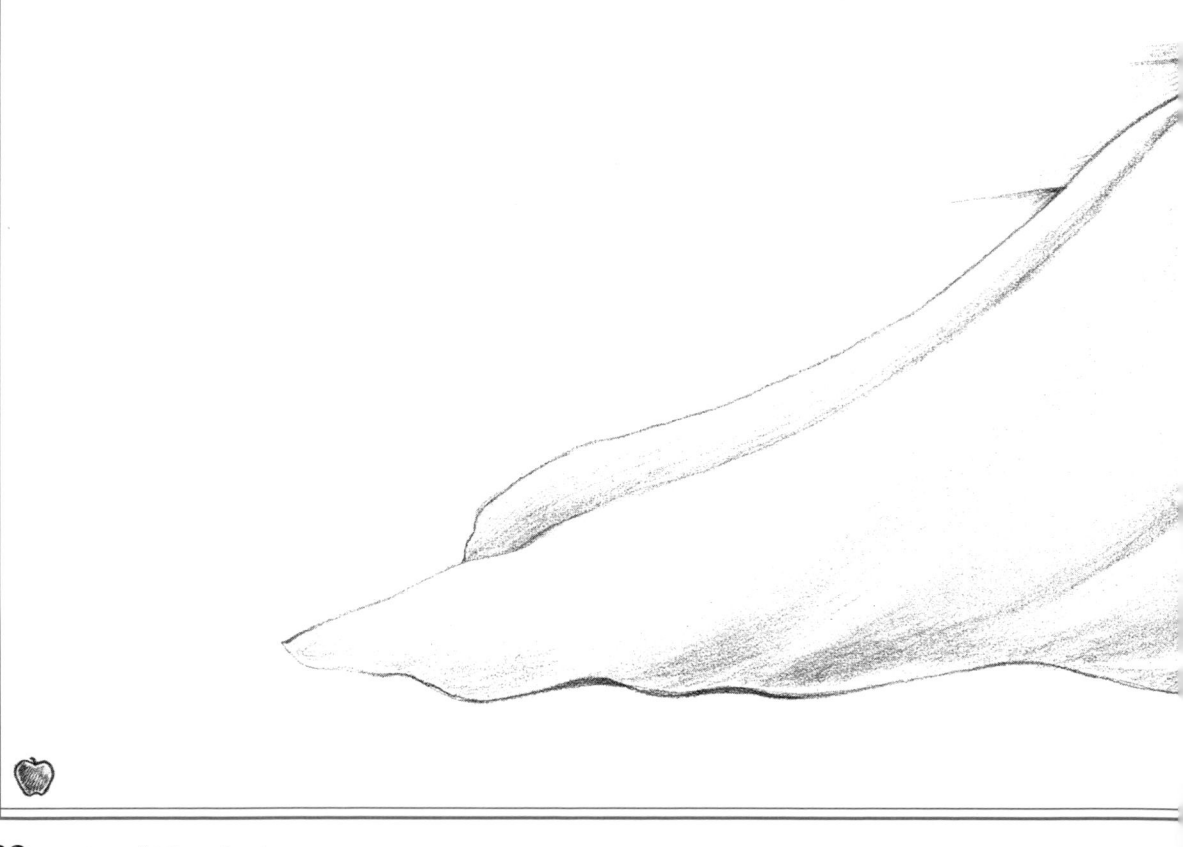

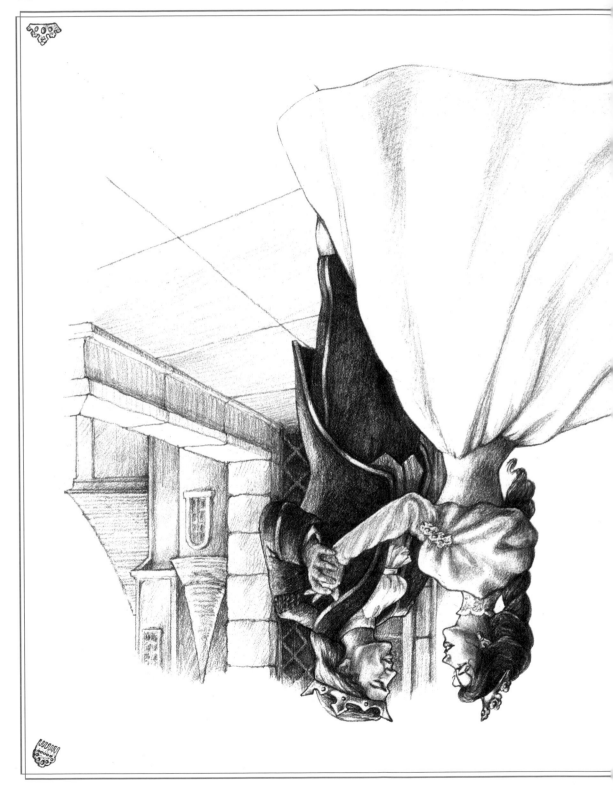